UP IN BUBBLES

Barbara Salsberg

ANNICK PRESS • TORONTO

Annick Press gratefully acknowledges the support of
The Canada Council and the Ontario Arts Council.

Cover photograph by Carrie Branovan

Canadian Catalogue in Publication Data
Salsberg, Barbara
     Up In Bubbles
ISBN 0 920236 37 5
1. Title.
PS8587 .A6296U75 JC813'.5'4 C79-094529-0
PZ7.S25Up

Annick Press
23 Homewood Avenue,
Willowdale, Ontario, Canada M2M 1K1

Printed in Canada by The Hunter Rose Company Limited

For my friends; Ellen, Ruth and Boots

"Oh, boy!" said Mr. McGrood, "I'm tired and hot and hungry and it's two hours 'til supper."

Mr. McGrood didn't like plowing. He didn't like haying either.

Actually, he didn't like most things.

Ellen McGrood was your age.

She was in the house again, looking out, scrubbing and daydreaming, with water all over the floor.

"I haven't even started dinner. I think we'll have bubble gum salad, baked gum and bubble gum jello today," she said. "First I have to find some of that gum, though."

"Definitely," said Granny, who was up on the wall.

Ellen practiced a speech before going out. "Gimme some of that gum!" she was going to say.

"Oh-oh," said Granny.

" 'Can I have some of your gum' then?" Granny still looked doubtful.

"Please," said Ellen as she went outside, but Peter and Karin had gone home.

Ellen was a little sad. She rarely had enough time to play with her friends.

Hey, they had left some gum on the ground. "Here comes a taste of dinner," said Ellen. "Dad will be surprised, I guess. He likes potato salad and meat balls. Oh, well."

Ellen chewed and chewed. "I'm very good at this," she said. Only at first she wasn't.

"Maybe if I inhale I'll get a bubble?" Ellen almost choked on the gum. Then a tiny fly got into her nose.

ACHOO! Sneezed Ellen and sailed up in the air.

"Hey, I think it works, watch me, watch me gooOOOOOO!"

She was too busy trying to land on her feet to notice the bubble in her mouth.

"Try, try again," Mr. McGrood would say when he was around, which was not often.

"Here goes," said Ellen.

Her bubble grew bigger and **Bigger** and BIGGER.
"Who can see with this thing in front of my nose!"
Ellen pushed and scrambled until she was inside the bubble.
"First I am going to Africa. No, make that China," she
said. Too bad Granny wasn't coming.

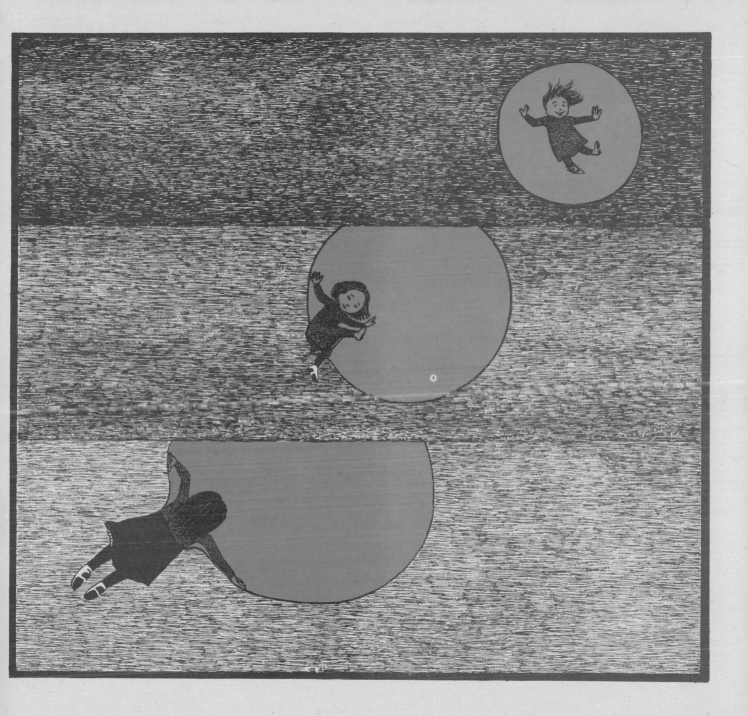

15

"Ellen!!" shouted Mr. McGrood, who was dirty, hungry and tired. "Ellen!!" He always shouted at Ellen. There was nobody else to shout at.

"Now, now," said Ellen's Granny up on the wall. "She went outside."

"What for?" shouted Mr. McGrood. "Where is my dinner?"

"She is going to Africa via China," said Ellen's Granny calmly. "And it wouldn't do you any harm if you took a little time off yourself."

"What for?" shouted Mr. McGrood again.

"Suit yourself," said Ellen's Granny.

"Africa! China!" said Mr. McGrood. "I ask you."

He went outside. Big people never believe anything, so he had to see for himself.

"I don't know why I'm doing this," said Mr. McGrood. Then he stepped on some sticky gum.

"Ellen!!" He peeled it off his shoe.

Then he spotted a little pink circle in the sky. Ellen didn't answer because she couldn't hear him. Also because she was trying to remember if she knew any Chinese.

19

"Yuk," said Mr. McGrood and then he tried a piece. "What will they think of next!" He made an angry mouth and a bubble slipped out.

"Oooooooh," moaned Mr. McGrood impatiently, and the bubble quickly grew bigger.

SPLAT!!! It popped all over his face, hair and ears.

"Yuk," shouted Mr. McGrood again, as he put it all back into his mouth and chewed some more.

All of a sudden, another bubble popped up and Mr. McGrood decided to be more patient this time. He blew and he blew sloooooowly and it grew bigger.

Mr. McGrood didn't want to go to China, or even as far as the gas station, but up-UP he went and he climbed inside his bubble for comfort.

"Wait a minute. How am I going to get down? Ellen will think of something. Otherwise she will be in trouble," said Mr. McGrood.

Ellen had just decided she would go to Africa and China via Beaver Valley where she knew the language.

"Hey, Dad, watch me. I'm diving," she called.

He watched. "What are you doing?" he shouted.

"Rolling in the sky. It's fun! I think I'm going to stay."

"You come down this minute!"

"Why?"

"Good question," said Mr. McGrood to himself. He saw that Ellen was happy. Come to think of it, he was having a VERY GOOD TIME himself. "Granny was right. This will do me good."

He looked around to see if there were any other families bubbling together at this hour. Nobody but Ellen and himself.

"Where do you want to go," asked Mr. McGrood with a smile on his face. He was hoping it wouldn't be Africa or the North Pole, as he just remembered that he hadn't eaten any dinner.

"Just anywhere," said Ellen, and they rolled, floated and tumbled in their bubbles all night.

Karin, Peter and their friends were walking near the river the next morning.

"Guess what? Kids in bubble gum," said Peter, pointing to the sky.

"Don't be silly," said a big friend, "people don't float in the sky like that."

"I think they do," said another big person, "and they may be in trouble. Shouldn't we save them?"

"Why?" said Karin, waving.

"Want some gum?" offered Peter and he peeled some out of his pocket.

"Absolutely not," said some of their friends.

But a few, including a dog called Boots and a duck named Irving, were already practicing bubble-blowing.

"I am good at outdoor sports," said Irving, and he was.

Unfortunately, it was a windy day. Just as they were meeting the McGroods in their bubbles a big gust of wind blew them all together in a sticky bundle in the sky, and they slowly floated down and …

— splash, a soft landing in the middle of the river.

"Don't worry about me. I can swim," said Irving, the duck. But the bubbles didn't burst and nobody was worried.

Just ahead of them there was a small town.

"Oh, no," said Boots, the dog, "I can't stand small towns. Too many dogs!"

"Where are we going?" Peter wanted to know.

"Tell you later, when I've decided," said Ellen, who was watching the water looking for surprises.

Bubbling along like this was a lot of fun. Everyone giggled and laughed.

The people in town saw them coming and they didn't know what to make of it. The whole pink mess looked unheard of. The mayor looked out the window and immediately declared an emergency. He appointed a committee. They called the police and the fire truck. They rang the church bells and sent out the rowing team.

35

But the rescue didn't work.

Ellen was still lying face down in her bubble.

"I'm watching out for the terrible river snake," she said.

"WHAT terrible river snake?"

"Who knows," said Ellen. "I'll take it home and keep it in our big barrel outside Dad's window." But they didn't see any snake.

37

pop POP Pop pop POP POP POP pop POP — they suddenly bumped into an island. Everyone was covered in bubble gum.

"Let's make a sticky parade," said Ellen.

"Yes, I'll be the clown," said Peter.

"Can I be a reindeer? " Boots wanted to know.

"No, you already are a dog," said Karin.

Mr. McGrood and Ellen pretended they were a marching band. After the parade they took off their shoes and socks and waded and skipped pebbles. Irving, the duck, was fishing.

"Let's see who can spit the farthest."

"This morning when I woke up I just knew it wasn't one of my good spitting days," said Karin.

Ellen found a bottle bobbing in the water. Granny would like it here, she thought.

Dear Granny,

We are on Sticky Island, it's so much fun. Please come. I'm sending some bubble gum to blow up.

Sincerely Yours,

Ellen

P.S. Could you bring some potato salad or at least strawberries for nine?

Ellen put the note and the gum into the bottle and threw it out into the river.

43

Ellen's Granny hated flying, but this was different.

The very next morning she arrived in the biggest bubble they had ever seen. Everyone cheered.

She spent a happy day with Ellen, her dad and their friends.

"Now that you found this special bubble gum, things will never be the same," smiled Granny.

And she was right!